*Vidia Meets Her Match*

# Vidia Meets Her Match

WRITTEN BY
### Kiki Thorpe

ILLUSTRATED BY
### Judith Holmes Clarke &
### Adrienne Brown

RANDOM HOUSE  NEW YORK

*Library of Congress Cataloging-in-Publication Data*

Thorpe, Kiki.

Vidia meets her match / written by Kiki Thorpe ;
illustrated by Judith Holmes Clarke & Adrienne Brown.

p.    cm.

At head of title: Fairies.

Summary: Vidia finds her status as the fastest fairy in Pixie Hollow
jeopardized by the arrival of a fast-flying newcomer named Wisp.

*ISBN 978-0-7364-2607-7 (pbk.)*

*[1. Fairies—Fiction. 2. Competition (Psychology)—Fiction. 3. Conduct of
life—Fiction. 4. Interpersonal relations—Fiction.] I. Clarke, Judith Holmes,
ill. II. Brown, Adrienne, ill. III. Title.*

*PZ7.T3974Vi 2010*

[Fic]—dc22                    2008048587

www.randomhouse.com/kids

Printed in the United States of America

10 9 8 7 6 5 4 3 2 1

## All About Fairies

IF YOU HEAD toward the second star on your right and fly straight on till morning, you'll come to Never Land, a magical island where mermaids play and children never grow up.

When you arrive, you might hear something like the tinkling of little bells. Follow that sound and you'll find Pixie Hollow, the secret heart of Never Land.

A great old maple tree grows in Pixie Hollow, and in it live hundreds of fairies and sparrow men. Some of them can do water magic, others can fly like the wind, and still others can speak to animals. You see, Pixie Hollow is the Never fairies' kingdom, and each fairy who lives there has a special, extraordinary talent.

Not far from the Home Tree, nestled in the branches of a hawthorn, is Mother Dove, the most magical creature of all. She sits on her egg, watching over the fairies, who in turn watch over her. For as long as Mother Dove's egg stays well and whole, no one in Never Land will ever grow old.

Once, Mother Dove's egg *was* broken. But we are not telling the story of the egg here. Now it is time for Vidia's tale. . . .

Vidia
Meets
Her
Match

# 1

"A LAUGH IS coming! A new fairy is on the way!"

The cry went up from a scout, who had spotted the glimmer from his tree-top perch. A harvest-talent fairy heard him. She passed the news to a butterfly herder, who shouted it to a garden-talent fairy. Soon, all around Pixie Hollow, fairies were aflutter with excitement.

The fast-flying-talent fairy Vidia was lounging on a branch of her sour-plum tree when the news reached her pointed ears.

"A new fairy, hmm?" Vidia said. She sat up and peeked through the leaves of the tree. She saw groups of fairies hurrying toward the Home Tree. Snippets of their conversation drifted up to her.

"Oh, I hope she'll be a grass-weaving-talent fairy!"

"We could really use another caterpillar herder."

"She's a mud talent, I'm sure. I can feel it in my wings."

Vidia rolled her eyes. She didn't care a shred about caterpillar herders or grass weavers or mud-talent fairies. The only fairies that interested her were fast fliers. But it had been ages since one of those had arrived in Pixie Hollow.

Still, Vidia couldn't help being curious. It was always an event when a new fairy arrived in Pixie Hollow. Besides, the sight of all the fairies flying quickly toward the courtyard made her want to race them there.

"I might as well go see the new fairy," she said to herself. She stood and flexed her wings. Then she sprang from the branch into the air.

Vidia zoomed down over the meadow. She flew so fast that the tips of the grass bent beneath her like treetops in the wind. She skirted the orchard and did a double loop around the dairy barn, just to scare the mice inside. A dairy talent came out and shouted at her. But Vidia didn't hear a word because the wind was rushing in her ears.

Moments later, she flew up to the Home Tree. The courtyard was empty except for a single sweeping-talent fairy. She was tidying up with a twig-handled broom. Vidia whipped by so fast that she stirred up a dust devil.

The sweeper chased the dust devil with her broom. "What's the rush, Vidia?" she snapped.

Vidia arched an eyebrow. "Haven't you heard the news?" she said.

"What news?" asked the sweeper.

Vidia smirked. Not only had she

flown faster than the other fairies—she'd flown faster than their gossip! In Pixie Hollow that was fast indeed.

"A new fairy is arriving today," she told the sweeper.

The fairy's eyes widened. "A new fairy? Today?" she cried. "But this place is a mess!" She began to scurry around the courtyard. She whisked her broom this way and that.

*How pitiful,* Vidia thought, watching her. *I'm glad I'm not a sweeping-talent fairy.* Of course, she knew that sweepers loved to sweep as much as she loved to fly. Still, sweeping seemed hideously boring.

Soon the others began to show up. The courtyard filled with fairies.

They were all laughing and chattering.

Vidia stood away from them. She leaned against a toadstool and folded her arms across her chest. *I wish the laugh would hurry up*, she thought. She was already sick of listening to the other fairies babble.

"There! I see it!" Tinker Bell cried, pointing at the sky.

The crowd hushed. High over their heads, the laugh was coasting in on a quick-moving breeze. When it passed the Home Tree, it dropped down. Just before it reached the courtyard, it exploded in a shimmering burst.

Everyone crowded closer, eager to get a look at the new fairy. But when the shimmers cleared, they saw . . . nothing.

The fairies stared at the empty spot where the new fairy should have been.

"Was it merely a hiccup?" someone asked.

At times babies' hiccups got caught on a breeze and floated all the way to Never Land. But these always vanished as soon as they arrived. Only a baby's first laugh could turn into a fairy.

"No, look! Up there!" cried Prilla.

The brand-new fairy was standing on a branch over their heads. She grinned down at them. At once, the crowd began to murmur.

"How in Never Land did she get up there?"

"She must have flown!"

"Without fairy dust? Her wings must be strong!"

Vidia took a closer look at the new fairy. If her wings really were that strong, she might be a fast flier after all.

*Someone new to race*, Vidia thought. *And someone new to beat.*

The fairy-dust-talent sparrow man

Terence flew up to the new arrival. He sprinkled fairy dust over her. Then she began to glow like the other fairies— bright yellow, edged with gold. She fanned her wings, feeling fairy-dust magic for the first time.

Then, with a quickness that made all the fairies gasp, she leaped from the branch. She darted to the ground and landed lightly in front of the crowd. Everyone quieted down. They waited for her to announce her name and talent.

"My name is Wisp," the new fairy declared. "I'm a fast-flying-talent fairy."

With a cheer, the fast fliers rushed forward to hug her. The rest of the fairies sighed and applauded.

"The name suits her," said the garden

talent Rosetta. Other fairies nodded. Wisp was tiny, with a shock of wild white hair like a dandelion puff. Even her voice was light and quick.

But Vidia didn't care about Wisp's name or what she looked like. It was Wisp's talent that interested her. She pushed her way to the front of the crowd. Vidia was taller than most fairies, and she towered over Wisp.

"Fly with you, darling," she said to the new fairy. "It seems you and I have a lot in common."

2

"Leave her alone, Vidia," said a fast flier named Leeta. She put a protective arm around Wisp.

Vidia raised her eyebrows and pretended to be surprised. "Can't I greet a member of my own talent, dearest?" she asked.

Leeta scowled. She turned to Wisp.

"You don't want to get mixed up with Vidia," she said. "She's trouble."

Wisp looked at Vidia again. Her eyes were filled with curiosity.

Vidia just shrugged. She knew that the other fairies didn't like her. Even the fast fliers usually steered clear of her, unless they had to work together to stir up breezes. But Vidia didn't care. She was faster than all of them put together. Who needed friends when you were the best?

Before Vidia could say more, Leeta led the new fairy away. "Come on, Wisp," Leeta said.

"Where are we going?" Wisp asked.

"To the hawthorn tree," said Leeta. "You want to meet Mother Dove, don't you?" Mother Dove was the magical bird who watched over the Never fairies.

As they flew away, Wisp glanced at Vidia one more time. Vidia heard her ask Leeta, "Why don't you like Vidia? Did she do something wrong?"

Vidia couldn't hear Leeta's answer. But she knew what it would be. Leeta would tell Wisp that Vidia had plucked feathers from Mother Dove. Plucking was illegal, of course. But that hadn't stopped Vidia.

Vidia wished Wisp hadn't left with Leeta so quickly. *The child has promise,* she thought. *With the right training, she might make a half-decent fast flier.* She decided to follow them to Mother Dove's tree.

As luck would have it, Leeta and Wisp were flying into the wind. Vidia usually hated headwinds because they slowed her down. But right now she was glad. The breeze carried Wisp and Leeta's conversation back to her.

"Why did she pluck the feathers?" she heard Wisp ask Leeta.

"All of Mother Dove's feathers are magical," Leeta told Wisp. "You know that, right?"

Wisp nodded. Like most fairies, she had arrived with some knowledge of Pixie Hollow.

"Well, Vidia ground up the feathers. She used them to make extra-powerful fairy dust so that she could fly faster," Leeta told her.

"Vidia has special dust to fly faster?" Wisp asked.

"Yes," said Leeta. "She's the fastest fairy in Pixie Hollow—and the most selfish."

Wisp and Leeta were now passing Havendish Stream. The noisy bubbling of the water drowned out their words. Vidia closed some of the distance between them. She didn't want to miss anything they were saying.

"What happened to the dust?" Wisp was asking when Vidia caught up.

"No one knows for sure," Leeta told her. "Some fairies say she still has it hidden in her home in the sour-plum tree. I heard that a fairy once tried to find it. When Vidia caught her, she grabbed her by the wings and threw her into Havendish Stream. She would have drowned if a water talent hadn't spotted her!"

*So that's what they're saying about me, is it?* Vidia thought with a chuckle. *Well, at least it keeps them away from my tree.*

Wisp flew silently for a moment.

Then she said, "I'd like to be the fastest fairy in Pixie Hollow. Wouldn't you?"

"Not if it means being like Vidia," Leeta huffed. Vidia couldn't see her face, but she could imagine its sour look. "When the scouts caught her stealing feathers, Queen Clarion grounded her for a month."

Leeta and Wisp both shuddered. For a fast flier, a whole month of not flying was unthinkable.

"But if you ask me, she got what she deserved," Leeta went on. "Vidia is heartless. She's never done a single kind thing in her life."

Vidia knew the other fairies didn't care for her. But it still stung to hear someone say it out loud.

Wisp and Leeta were nearing the hawthorn tree now. Vidia slowed down. If one of the scouts who guarded the tree spotted her, she'd be in trouble. Because of the plucking, Vidia was no longer allowed near Mother Dove's nest.

But Vidia knew a secret way to the tree through an old groundhog tunnel. She wanted to hear what Mother Dove said to Wisp. Mother Dove often knew fairies even better than they knew themselves.

Vidia made a wide loop around the tree and flew to the tunnel entrance. She had cleverly hidden it with a large pumice stone. The stone looked heavy, but it was actually as light as a feather. Vidia lifted it with ease.

She took a deep breath, then darted in. "Ugh," she said as a few grains of dirt fell into her hair. Like most winged creatures, Vidia was happiest in the sky. The narrow tunnel made her feel trapped. She flew as quickly as she could, shivering when the tips of roots brushed against her wings.

The tunnel ended at the hawthorn tree. Vidia checked to make sure no one was watching. Then she zipped up the back of the trunk. She hid herself among the leaves.

Mother Dove's nest was on one of the low branches. Vidia could see Wisp already there, perched on the edge.

"Welcome to Pixie Hollow," cooed Mother Dove. "We're glad to have you."

Wisp stood straighter, and her glow brightened. Mother Dove had that effect on fairies.

Mother Dove studied Wisp. "You're afraid of nothing. I can see that," she said. "You're as quick as the wind—and just as bold. The most fearless flier we've ever seen."

Vidia peeked through the leaves. Wisp was beaming. But Mother Dove looked more worried than happy.

"Wisp . . . ," Mother Dove began. She hesitated.

"Yes?" said Wisp.

Mother Dove looked as if she was about to say something. Then she seemed to change her mind. "Please just try to be careful," she told the new fairy.

Wisp laughed. "All right, Mother Dove."

Vidia had heard enough. She hurried back to the tunnel. As she flew down through the darkness, Mother Dove's words rang in her mind: *Quick as the wind . . . bold . . . the most fearless flier.*

*Could Wisp be faster than me?* Vidia wondered.

She had to find out.

Vidia guessed that Wisp would return to the Home Tree. So she flew straight there. She hid behind one of the tree's twisted roots and waited.

It wasn't long before Wisp and Leeta came flying back. "I have to go now," Leeta told Wisp. "But I'll show you your room right after lunch."

Vidia waited as Leeta said good-bye. When Wisp was alone in the courtyard, she flew out from her hiding place. Vidia landed right in front of the new fairy.

"Vidia!" Wisp gasped.

"There's nothing to be afraid of, child," Vidia said with a smirk. "I'm not going to eat you."

"I wasn't afraid," Wisp said. She looked Vidia in the eye. "You just startled me, that's all. What are you doing here?"

"Well, I've been having such a dull day," Vidia said casually. "I said to myself, 'Why don't I find that new little fairy and see if she wants to race.'"

Wisp's whole face lit up. "Race? With you? I'd love to!" she cried. "I hear you're the fastest fairy in Pixie Hollow."

"Mmm. Well, we'll see, won't we?" said Vidia.

Wisp's wings were already humming. "Where should we race?" she asked.

Vidia looked around. "From here to that tree," she decided. She pointed to a peach tree at the edge of the orchard. "To finish, touch the peach hanging from that low branch. Ready?"

Wisp nodded. The two got on their marks.

"Set . . . ," said Vidia.

They spread their wings.

"Go!"

3

THE TWO FAIRIES shot into the air. Right
away, Vidia pulled ahead. But she didn't
want to win too quickly. She wanted to
see how Wisp flew first.

Vidia slowed her pace a little. Wisp
was fast. But her flying was wild.

*She hasn't learned to use her wings yet,*
Vidia thought. Of course, this wasn't

unusual. Wisp had just arrived, after all.

Halfway to the peach tree, Vidia sped up. To her surprise, Wisp sped up, too. She pulled ahead of Vidia.

Vidia poured on more speed. Wisp did the same. They were flying wing and wing now. Wisp was so out of control that her wings were wobbling. But she just kept going faster.

As they closed in on the peach tree, Vidia was less than a fairy's length ahead of Wisp. She touched the peach and shot on past. A half-second later, Wisp smacked into the peach so hard she knocked it from the tree.

Vidia came to a stop, breathing hard. She looked down. Wisp was on the ground, stuck headfirst in the fruit.

Vidia gave a shriek of laughter. She flew down, grabbed Wisp's ankles, and pulled her out.

Wisp's face was flushed. Peach juice dribbled off the ends of her hair. But she was grinning. "That was fun!" she exclaimed.

"Not bad for your first race," Vidia said. The truth was, it was the closest race she'd had in a long time. Wisp was surprisingly fast.

*Not as fast as me*, Vidia thought. *But faster than most in our talent.*

"Don't let that juice dry on your wings," Vidia told her. She started to fly away.

"Wait!" said Wisp. "Where are you going?"

Vidia glanced back at her. "Home, dear child."

Wisp's mouth turned down in dismay. "But . . . but I thought we would fly together," she said.

Vidia shrugged. The race was over. She had proved that she was still the fastest. She didn't see any reason to spend more time with Wisp.

But Wisp chased her. "I was hoping we would be friends," she said.

Vidia was so surprised, she stopped in midair. She turned around and stared at Wisp. "Why would you want to be friends with me?" she asked.

"Because you're the fastest," Wisp said, as if the answer were obvious. "I want to be friends with the best fairy."

Vidia arched an eyebrow. "Really? And what makes you think I'd want to be friends with you?" she asked.

Now it was Wisp's turn to look surprised. "Why wouldn't you?" she said.

"What do you suppose the other fairies would say if they saw you flying with me?" Vidia asked. "What would Leeta think?"

Wisp made a face. "Who cares? Leeta is bossy, and she's boring. She's not even that fast," she said.

Vidia had to smile. She was starting to like this odd little fairy.

Wisp fluttered up into the air and did a little spin. "I want to go fast, fast, fast!" she exclaimed. "I want to be the fastest thing in all Never Land!"

Vidia watched her, amused. She'd felt the same way when she was a new fairy. In fact, she still felt that way.

Wisp spread her arms wide, as if to hug the sky. Then, suddenly, her eyes closed and she tipped backward. Her wings stopped fluttering. She dropped like a stone toward the ground.

It happened so quickly that Vidia barely had time to react. Had Wisp just fainted? Had the race been too much for her?

Then, just as suddenly, Wisp opened her wings. She caught herself a few inches above the ground. "Now, *that* was fast!" she called up to Vidia.

Vidia blinked. She couldn't believe it. Wisp had fallen . . . for *fun*?

Wisp zipped back up to Vidia. "So, what do you say? Want to race again?" she asked.

A smile slowly stretched across Vidia's face. Wisp was turning out to be one of the strangest fairies she had ever met—and one of the most interesting.

"Let's go," she said.

# 4

In the days that followed, Vidia and Wisp raced many more times. Their flying was so fast that they created a gust of wind wherever they went—much to the annoyance of the other fairies.

They blew all the clothes off the laundry lines. They scared a herd of woolly caterpillars. And one day, they caused such a breeze that it tipped over all the leaf-boats on Havendish Stream. The queen was so angry, she grounded them for a whole day.

Vidia didn't care. She couldn't remember the last time she'd had so much fun.

One morning, a week after Wisp had arrived, Vidia awoke in her feather bed. The light coming in the window was thin and grayish. Through her spiderweb curtains, she could see dawn turning the sky pink.

Vidia sat up and stretched. Her shoulders felt sore, but in a good way. The day before, she and Wisp had flown all the way around Pixie Hollow. Wisp had shown off by trying to race a hornet. She'd almost gotten stung!

Vidia laughed, thinking about it. She wondered where they'd race today.

Vidia climbed out of her bed. Then she reached under it and pulled out her box of special fairy dust—the dust made from Mother Dove's feathers. It was the first thing she did every morning.

The box was locked with six padlocks. Vidia checked each one. When she was sure they were locked tight, she put the box back under the bed. Vidia didn't use the special dust often. Terence sprinkled each fairy every day with a cup of regular fairy dust. That was enough to keep her flying fast. But she stored a pinch of special dust in a pouch at her waist, in case she needed it. She liked to know that she could be even faster whenever she wanted to be.

Vidia had just stood up when she heard a knock on her door. "Who could that be?" she said with a scowl. She didn't like visitors.

She unbolted the door and opened it a hair. Wisp was standing on the twig outside. "Ready to race?" she asked.

"Dear child, it's the crack of dawn. I haven't even had tea," Vidia said.

"I can wait while you get ready," said Wisp. Her gaze slipped past Vidia into her house.

Vidia hesitated. She almost never let anyone inside. Then again, Wisp was her friend. At least, she was the closest thing to a friend Vidia had ever had.

With a sigh, she opened the door wider. "Don't touch anything," she grumbled as Wisp flew inside.

Wisp's eyes darted around. While Vidia had a whole tree to herself, she lived mostly in one room. But what an amazing room it was! The ceiling soared high overhead. The walls were painted to look like the sky. Windows gave her a view in every direction. Even when she was indoors, Vidia liked to feel as if she were flying.

"This is so much better than my room in the Home Tree!" exclaimed Wisp. She reached out toward one of Vidia's bedposts. "Are these—"

"Hawk feathers. I said, don't touch anything," Vidia snapped.

"Hawk feathers," Wisp repeated. Her voice was full of awe. "Have you flown with a hawk?"

Vidia rolled her eyes. "Of course not. Hawks eat fairies. Or didn't you know that?"

Secretly, Vidia longed to fly alongside a hawk. Hawks were powerful and regal— they owned the sky. But she didn't dare. She'd taken the feathers from a hawk's nest while its owner was off hunting.

"Oh," Wisp said. "I thought you might have." She no longer looked impressed.

"I did pluck a feather from the Golden Hawk once," Vidia said quickly. She didn't want Wisp to think she was a coward.

"Really?" Wisp's eyes lit up. She looked around the room. "Where is it?"

"I don't have it," said Vidia. "We were taking it to Kyto the dragon in exchange for his help in saving Pixie Hollow. But it was lost on the way."

"You were going to give it away?" Wisp asked in disbelief. "I'd have kept it."

Vidia had never thought of keeping the Golden Hawk's feather. But now she wished she had. She, Prilla, and Rani had needed the feather to give to Kyto, but in the end it had been lost anyway. She might as well have kept it.

For the first time, Vidia felt she had been cheated out of her feather.

Wisp was still fluttering around the

room. She examined Vidia's collection of feathers so closely that her breath ruffled them. She poked into bowls on the shelves and tried to peek through the cracked door of a cupboard. After a few minutes Vidia began to get annoyed. Wisp was awfully nosy.

"Did you really pluck feathers from Mother Dove?" Wisp asked suddenly.

"What?" Vidia was startled. Most fairies were too embarrassed to mention Mother Dove's feathers to her. But even more surprising than the question was the way Wisp had asked it. She didn't sound angry or scornful. Just curious.

Wisp waited for an answer.

"I did," Vidia said. "Because it was . . . necessary." This wasn't exactly true. It hadn't been necessary to hurt Mother Dove. But it was easier for Vidia to tell herself that it had been.

Wisp nodded, as if this answer made perfect sense to her.

"Shall we go now?" Vidia asked. She was tired of talking about feathers and plucking.

"Don't you want your tea?" Wisp asked.

Vidia gave her a tight-lipped smile. "I guess I'm not thirsty after all," she said.

Outside, Vidia and Wisp crisscrossed Havendish Stream, looking for a place to race.

"How about a sprint from the mill

to the dairy barn?" Vidia suggested.

"Nah." Wisp shook her head.

They flew by the gardens. Rosetta was carefully digging up a dandelion that had gone to seed. Vidia whipped past her, spreading the seeds all over Rosetta's garden.

"Vidia!" Rosetta yelled. She shook her fist.

Vidia laughed. She flew back to Wisp. "Let's race over all the gardens. We'll drive those silly garden talents crazy," she said.

Wisp sighed. "Boring."

Vidia was starting to lose patience. "Well, where do you want to race?" she snapped.

"I'm not sure," said Wisp. "I just

want to do something different." She stared into the distance.

All at once, a gleam came into Wisp's eyes. "Do you think you could fly faster than a wave?" she asked Vidia.

"A wave?" Vidia followed Wisp's gaze. Beyond Pixie Hollow, she could see the blue waters of the Mermaid Lagoon.

Vidia studied the waves. They rolled lazily to the shore and gently broke on the sand.

"Of course I can," she told Wisp.

Wisp grinned. "Come on. Prove it!" she said. She took off for the lagoon. Vidia followed.

When they got there, the two fairies flew out over the ocean. The waves looked much bigger here than they had from Pixie Hollow. And they were traveling much faster.

"So we'll pick a wave and race it in," Vidia said. "Right?"

There was no answer. Vidia turned. Wisp was diving straight toward the water.

Vidia dove after her. "What are you doing?" she asked Wisp. They were now just inches above the surf.

"It's more exciting down here," Wisp told her.

"Are you out of your mind? If a wave catches you, you'll drown!" Vidia said.

"All the more reason to fly fast," Wisp replied.

Before Vidia could think of an answer, a huge wave rose behind them.

Vidia gasped. "Fly!" she screamed.

She took off toward the shore. The wave was like an enormous beast. She could feel it bearing down on her. Its foamy crest curled over her head, as if it were trying to grab her.

She beat her wings as hard as she could. But with each flap they seemed to feel heavier. With a sense of dread, she

realized that her wings *were* getting heavier. Spray from the wave was soaking them, making it hard to fly.

Vidia's heart was in her throat. Any second now, the wave would swallow her!

The wave broke with a deafening roar. With her last bit of strength, Vidia pulled ahead of it. She threw herself onto the dry sand. The thin, white edge of the water lapped at her feet before pulling back into the ocean.

Vidia lay in the sand, panting. She knew she couldn't stay there for long. The next wave might be even bigger.

As soon as she'd caught her breath, she flew farther up the beach.

It was only then that she remembered Wisp. Vidia looked around.

Down the beach, she spotted something jumping around. It was Wisp—she was trying to fly, but she was covered from head to toe in sand from the crash landing.

Hopping and flapping like a baby chick, Wisp made her way over to Vidia. "Wasn't that fun?" she exclaimed.

Vidia's mouth fell open. "Fun? Dear child, we were almost *killed*!"

"That's what made it so exciting!" Wisp said. "We wouldn't have flown so fast otherwise. I think it was our best race yet." She jumped around, trying to shake the sand from her wings.

*She's absolutely fearless*, thought Vidia. She felt a twinge of envy.

"What's wrong?" Wisp asked when

she saw Vidia's face. "Didn't you have fun?"

"It was . . ." Vidia stopped herself from saying "terrifying." She couldn't allow Wisp to think she had been afraid. "Thrilling," she finished.

As soon as the words were out, Vidia realized they were true. It *had* been thrilling. The most thrilling race ever.

"And we learned something," Wisp said.

"What is that?" asked Vidia.

Wisp grinned. "Now we know we can fly faster than a wave," she said.

5

THE NEXT MORNING, Vidia was eager to race again. When Wisp didn't show up at her door, Vidia flew to the Home Tree to look for her. Finally, Vidia spotted her. Wisp was perched on a far branch of the Home Tree. She was talking to a group of keyhole-talent fairies.

*Keyhole talents? Why would Wisp bother*

*with them?* Vidia wondered. She watched as the keyhole talents laughed at something Wisp had said.

Vidia had just started to fly over to them when she heard someone call her name. She turned and saw Tinker Bell.

"Vidia, wait!" Tinker Bell cried. She was flapping her wings furiously to try to catch up.

Vidia was surprised. She and Tinker Bell weren't exactly friends. In fact, they usually avoided each other. She wondered why Tink was so anxious to see her now.

Tink drew up next to her. She was huffing and puffing. A few blond hairs had fallen loose from her ponytail. "I've been looking all over for you," she told Vidia.

"And now you've found me. What a shame," Vidia said. She liked to try to rile Tink up. Tink was known for having a short temper.

But she didn't rise to the bait this time. "Listen, Vidia," she said. "A phoenix flower caught fire near Spring Meadow. The pots-and-pans talents are filling buckets at the stream to help stop the blaze. But we can't carry water there fast enough. We need help."

"Help?" Vidia drawled. She raised an eyebrow. "But, darling, *you're* the great inventor. Why don't you just invent some *thingy* and save the day?"

"There isn't time!" Tink told her. "We need fast fliers. Will you help us?"

"Me?" Vidia laughed. "Dearest, *you*

might like to get muddy with the water talents. But I have better things to do."

"You mean racing with Wisp?" Tink asked scornfully.

"Maybe," Vidia said with a shrug.

"I saw you racing in the Mermaid Lagoon yesterday," Tink told her. "It was foolish to fly so close to the water. You could have drowned."

"But we didn't, did we?" Vidia said. She didn't think it was any of Tink's business where she flew.

Just then, a loud cheer went up from the keyhole-talent fairies. Vidia and Tink looked over and saw Wisp showing off. She had jumped off the branch with one wing tied behind her back.

They watched as Wisp fluttered

unevenly to the ground like a broken maple seed. She barely managed to avoid landing on her head.

Tink frowned. "Wisp does stupid things," she said. "Dangerous, stupid things. I don't know why you fly with her. I guess you want to prove you're faster than she is, don't you?"

"How sweet of you to be concerned, Tink, darling," Vidia said. "But I already know that I'm faster than she is. I fly with Wisp because she's the only interesting fairy in Pixie Hollow. Now, if you'll excuse me . . ."

Tink's round cheeks flushed with anger. "You are so selfish!" she snapped. "If Pixie Hollow burns, you can blame yourself."

"Phoenix flowers have caught fire before, darling," Vidia said with a wave of her hand. "I'm sure you'll all be able to deal with it."

As Vidia flew off, a feeling of annoyance crept over her. Why had Tink tried to warn her about Wisp? *It should be the other way around*, Vidia thought. *After all, everyone knows I'm the dangerous fairy.*

"I thought we could race in the forest today," Vidia said as she and Wisp flew away from the Home Tree.

"That sounds fun. I haven't been there before," Wisp said.

Vidia was relieved that Wisp didn't want to race in the lagoon again. Her shoulders ached from their race the day before. She wasn't sure she'd be able to outfly another wave.

Vidia led Wisp toward the tall trees beyond Pixie Hollow. As they passed over Spring Meadow, Vidia smelled smoke. "Slow down," she told Wisp.

Wisp frowned. "Slow down? Why?"

They flew over a small hill and saw the fire. It spread across one edge of the meadow.

"What's going on?" Wisp asked.

"A phoenix flower has flared up," Vidia explained. "It happens every few years. The plant bursts into flame. Then it has to burn all the way to the ground before it can grow again. Unfortunately, it sets all the plants around it on fire, too."

Vidia had slowed her pace to a crawl. This fire was bigger than usual, she noticed. Even from a distance, she could hear it crackle and feel its heat. But she could also see fairies carrying pots and buckets of water from the stream. It looked as though they had it under control.

Wisp had already lost interest in the fire. She fidgeted. She sighed. Her toes tapped the air.

Finally, she turned to Vidia and asked, "*Why* are we flying so slowly?"

"Our wings send up a breeze," Vidia said. "If we fly too fast, we'll fan the flames." She might not be helping to put out the fire, but she didn't want to burn down Pixie Hollow, either.

After a few minutes—and several more impatient sighs from Wisp—they left the meadow behind. "It should be all right now," Vidia told her.

With a gasp of relief, Wisp shot ahead. Vidia chased her all the way to the forest.

Compared to the bright light and heat of the meadow, the forest was cool and dim. Wisp flitted from tree to tree.

"This is a great place to race!" she said.

"We can fly around these pinecones like an obstacle course," Vidia suggested. She began to plot their path through the branches of the pine tree. "We'll start here, then loop here—"

Wisp cut her off. "What's that?" she asked.

"What's what?" asked Vidia.

"That sound."

Vidia listened. She heard a dull thunk, like something hitting wood. It was followed by shrill squawks and gobbles.

"It's just the Lost Boys," Vidia said with a shrug.

"What are Lost Boys?" Wisp asked.

"Clumsy brats," said Vidia. "They are Peter Pan's friends. They're probably out hunting in the forest with their bows and arrows. Though it sounds like they're hitting more trees than squirrels," she observed.

"Let's go find them!" said Wisp. She started to dart ahead.

Vidia grabbed Wisp's shoulder and pulled her back. "Find them? Whatever for? They'll only try to catch you with their grubby hands," she said.

Wisp hopped onto a tree branch. She perched there, listening as the Lost Boys sent up another ruckus. "They

make such funny sounds. Are they fast?"
she asked Vidia.

"No, they're the slowest, clumsiest
creatures in all of Never Land," Vidia
told her.

"Oh. Well, I still want to see them."
Wisp flew off in the direction of the
sound. This time, Vidia sighed and
followed her.

# 6

Vidia and Wisp flew through the forest until they came to a clearing. A pack of boys dressed in dirty fur suits stood in the middle of it. They all held bows and arrows.

"Ready!" shouted the Lost Boy named Slightly. The boys raised their bows to their shoulders.

"Aim!" shouted Slightly. "Fire!"

A volley of arrows flew through the air. Vidia saw that the boys weren't hunting. They were shooting at a target painted onto a tree trunk.

With a thunk, one arrow hit the bull's-eye. The rest landed all over the tree. One flew into the bushes.

"I win!" squealed Slightly.

"You do not! I win," said Nibs. He jabbed his thumb at his chest. "Was my arrow that hit the bull's-eye."

"Was not. Was mine!" Slightly ran over and yanked the arrow from the target. "See? It's got red-tailed hawk feathers on it."

"Those aren't from a hawk. They're chicken feathers," said Cubby.

Vidia rolled her eyes. She had no use for the Lost Boys—or any Clumsies, for that matter. "Now you've seen them," she said to Wisp. "Can we go?"

"Wait! What are those?" Wisp asked, pointing.

"Arrows, of course," Vidia said. Sometimes she forgot how little Wisp knew.

"Arrows," Wisp murmured, her eyes widening.

Down on the ground, the boys were still arguing. "It could've been my arrow," said one of the twins. "See, mine have red feathers, too."

"Hey, that's mine!" cried his brother. "You stole that from me!" He tried to grab the arrow out of his twin's hand.

Before long, the two were rolling in the dirt.

"Maybe we should all go again," Cubby suggested. "Since we don't know whose arrow it is, I mean."

"Good idea! Let's go again!" the boys cried.

Wisp turned to Vidia. "Let's find out if we can fly faster than an arrow!" she said.

Vidia gave her a wry smile. "You think they won't notice if we line up alongside their arrows? 'Oh, don't mind us,'" she said, pretending to talk to a Lost Boy. "'We're just having a race.'"

Wisp shook her head. "No, we'll fly from here to that rock." She pointed a path directly across the target. "We'll

leave at the same time as the arrows."

Vidia stopped smiling. "But we could get hit," she said.

"Not if we fly faster than the arrows." Wisp looked at Vidia and added, "You aren't afraid, are you?" She didn't say it in a mean way. She said it as if it was the first time such a thing had ever occurred to her.

"Of course not!" Vidia scoffed. Her? Afraid? She was the fastest, bravest fairy in Pixie Hollow!

"I didn't think so," Wisp said cheerfully. "You and I are just alike. We're not afraid of anything."

"Ready?" shouted Slightly.

The fairies crouched into starting positions. Vidia's mouth felt dry. She glanced over at the Lost Boys. They were fitting arrows to their bows.

"Aim," said Slightly. The boys raised their bows to their shoulders. Vidia focused on the rock ahead. *Pretend it's just a normal race*, she told herself.

"Fire!"

The arrows flew from the bows. At the same moment, the two fairies shot through the air. Vidia didn't once look at the arrows. All she thought about was reaching the other side.

It was over in a split second. Vidia landed on the rock. "Ha! Faster than an arrow!" she cried triumphantly.

There was no answer.

"Wisp?" said Vidia. She turned to look behind her. Wisp wasn't there.

Vidia whipped around to look at the tree. Her insides went cold. Wisp was pinned to one of the target's red rings. The shaft of an arrow jutted straight out of her side.

The Lost Boys spotted Wisp at the same moment.

"Look, I shot a fairy!" Slightly cried. "Wait till I tell Peter!"

"No, I shot it. It's mine!" said Nibs.

"Is not!"

"Is so!"

Vidia flew closer. She could hardly bear to look at Wisp.

But then, to her amazement, Wisp wriggled! She tugged at her clothes. The arrow had only pierced Wisp's dress!

Vidia glanced over at the Lost Boys.

She wanted to help Wisp. But she didn't want the boys to catch her.

As Vidia hovered, Wisp gave her dress a fierce yank. The fabric ripped, and Wisp pulled free.

"Look, the fairy! It's getting away!"

The Lost Boys all tried to grab her. But Wisp darted through their hands.

She stuck out her tongue, turned a somersault in the air, and flew away laughing.

"You're right," she said as she and Vidia flew off. "Those Lost Boys are the slowest, clumsiest creatures I've ever seen." She fingered the hole in her dress and added, "But they gave us a great race."

Wisp flew ahead. Shaking her head, Vidia followed.

7

THE NEXT DAY, Vidia didn't see Wisp. She didn't show up at Vidia's house in the morning. Nor did Vidia see her flying anywhere near the Home Tree.

Vidia wondered if the close call with the arrow had scared Wisp. Maybe she was taking a day off to recover.

It didn't occur to Vidia to drop by

Wisp's room to see how she was feeling. Vidia never did such things. She spent the day flying around Pixie Hollow at an easy pace (easy, that is, for a fast-flying-talent fairy). It had been a while since she'd flown alone, and she enjoyed it. Still, she found that she missed Wisp.

But bright and early the following morning, the wild-haired fairy was at Vidia's front door.

"I see you're feeling better," Vidia said when she saw her.

"Better?" Wisp looked confused.

"After the arrow," Vidia added.

"Oh, that!" Wisp laughed. "Yes, I've never felt better. I flew halfway across Never Land yesterday."

"Halfway across Never Land?" Vidia

said. "That's not possible. Never Land is enormous. No fairy can fly across it—not with just a day's worth of fairy dust."

A look of uncertainty flashed across Wisp's face. "Er, maybe it wasn't that far after all," she said quickly. "But the great news is, I found the perfect place for us to race. Come on!" Grabbing Vidia's wrist, she dragged her into the air.

"Where are we going?" Vidia asked.

"You'll see," Wisp said.

They flew over the forest until the trees began to thin. The landscape turned hard and rocky. Soon the only plants they saw were grumble scrub and raindrop cactuses. They had reached Never Land's desert.

Ahead of them, the land dropped

away in a steep cliff. Vidia and Wisp stopped at the edge of a rocky canyon. Far below, Vidia could see a thin trickle of water winding along the canyon floor. A pair of hawks wheeled in the sky above.

"The Screaming Cliffs," Vidia told Wisp as one of the hawks let loose a piercing shriek. Its scream echoed off the canyon walls. Vidia shivered. "What are we doing here?" she asked.

"We're going to race, of course!" Wisp said. "From the top of the cliffs down to the bottom."

"But the hawks . . ." Vidia's words trailed off. She stared at the hawks circling over the canyon.

"I know! I've always wanted to fly with them. Haven't you?" Wisp said.

Of course, Vidia had always longed to fly with a hawk. But she knew Wisp's idea was crazy. If the hawks caught sight of them, they would be lunch. "My child, you're being stu—"

"On your mark!" Wisp exclaimed. "Get set. . . . Go!"

Wisp dove off the cliff.

"She's going to get herself killed," Vidia said. But she dove after Wisp.

Vidia felt herself lifted by the air currents. For a second, she forgot about Wisp. In the clear, bright sunlight, all her senses seemed sharper. The wind whipped through her hair. It ruffled the wings on her back.

At that moment, she knew how it felt to be a hawk. And, oh—it was glorious!

She glanced over at Wisp to see if she was enjoying it, too. But the young fairy's face was grim. A second later, Vidia saw why. There was a hawk on her tail!

Vidia felt the air around her change.

She saw another hawk come barreling out of the sky. It was headed right for her!

Vidia looked for a place to hide. But the cliff walls were smooth. Her only choice was straight down.

Vidia sped toward the canyon floor, fighting the air currents. When she glanced over her shoulder, she saw the hawk fold its wings. It was going into free fall!

Vidia snatched the pouch of extra-powerful fairy dust from her waist. Her fingers fumbled with the knot. The hawk closed in on her, its talons spread.

She finally managed to tear the bag open. She emptied it over herself. At once, she felt energy surge through her

wings. With a few quick strokes, Vidia shot ahead.

The hawk's claws closed on air. It screamed in frustration.

Vidia was flying so fast, she couldn't control her landing. The ground rose in front of her. She crashed headlong into some bushes. The last things she heard were leaves tearing and twigs snapping.

And then everything went dark.

# 8

When Vidia came to, she was lying in a wild rosebush at the edge of the creek. One of her wings was bent awkwardly under her. Her head throbbed where she'd hit it on a branch.

Vidia listened for the cries of the hawks. All was quiet. She carefully poked her head out of the rosebush. Far away, she could see two dark dots in the sky. The hawks had moved off to hunt in another part of the canyon.

Vidia climbed out of the bush. She was bruised and scraped all over. But she wasn't worried about that now. "Wisp!" she called. "Are you here?"

The only answer was the burbling of the creek.

She flew to the other side and called, "Wisp! Wisp!" In the massive canyon, she felt smaller than a speck of sand. Even her voice was too tiny to echo.

Vidia crossed the stream a few more times. There was no sign of Wisp.

With a sinking feeling, Vidia realized her friend had been caught. After all, Vidia had only been able to escape by using her special fairy dust. Without the extra power, Wisp didn't stand a chance.

"That stupid little fairy!" Vidia murmured. She was angry at Wisp for her crazy tricks. But it was terrible to think she'd lost her friend.

As she hovered, Vidia heard a rustle behind her. She spun around.

With a wild yell, Wisp came charging out of the bushes. Her white hair was sticking out in every direction like a lion's mane.

"Did I scare you?" she cried in delight.

"Wisp!" Vidia was so relieved to see the little fairy that her wings gave out. She plopped down in the dirt. "I thought you were—"

"A hawk's dinner?" Wisp laughed. "Nope. He couldn't catch me. He tried hard, though."

"But how did you . . ." Vidia didn't finish her question. She didn't need to. Wisp had outraced the hawk, plain and simple. And she had done it without the help of extra-powerful fairy dust.

That meant that Wisp was without a doubt the fastest fairy in Pixie Hollow. And maybe in the world. Vidia's relief turned to dismay.

"Is something the matter, Vidia?" Wisp asked.

"I have to go," Vidia told her. "I . . ." Vidia was too upset to even make up an excuse. She quickly flew away.

"Wait!" Wisp called to her. "Where

are you going?" Vidia didn't answer.

Vidia flew back to Pixie Hollow.

She had never cared that the other fairies didn't like her. She'd always known she was better than they were. After all, she was the fastest fairy in Pixie Hollow!

But if she was only the second fastest, then what?

Vidia knew the answer—she was nothing. "Selfish and heartless," she said, remembering Leeta's words. "And friendless, too," she added to herself.

Vidia's head was hung so low that she didn't see the other fairy until she bumped into her.

"Whoops! I— Oh, it's you," Tinker Bell said when she saw Vidia. Tink's leaf dress was soaked, and her face was streaked with soot. "We put out the fire, no thanks to—"

Tink broke off when she saw the look on Vidia's face. "What's wrong?" she asked, startled.

"Leave me alone," Vidia said. She flew around Tink.

Tink noticed Vidia's bruises. "You hurt yourself," she said. "Should I get a nursing-talent fairy?"

"I said, leave me alone," snapped Vidia. She started back toward her sour-plum tree.

"She won, didn't she?" Tink asked.

"What?" Vidia turned to look at Tinker Bell.

Tink nodded. "That's it. Wisp beat you in a race. You're pretty upset," she said. "She must have beaten you by a lot."

"Mind your own business," Vidia told Tink. She felt more miserable than ever. It was bad enough that anyone had seen her like this. But it was worse that it was Tink. She knew Tink would enjoy rubbing it in.

Sure enough, as Vidia flew home, Tink followed her. Vidia waited for Tink to make fun of her. But instead, Tink looked concerned.

"Just because Wisp is faster doesn't mean that she's better, Vidia," Tink told her. "There's more to flying than being fast."

Vidia stopped and opened her mouth. She wanted to say something mean, something really stinging. But she couldn't find the words.

Finally, she just shook her head. "No, there isn't," she said sadly.

They had reached the sour-plum tree.

"Go away, Tink," Vidia said. She turned to open the door.

Vidia's eyes widened. The door was already open. Someone was inside!

9

Vidia pushed open the door, with Tink on her heels.

"Wisp!" they both exclaimed.

Wisp looked up. She quickly hid something behind her back.

"What are you doing here?" Vidia asked.

"I just, er, wanted to see if you were

all right," Wisp said. Vidia could tell she was lying. Wisp's normally bright glow had turned a murky yellow.

Tink narrowed her eyes. "What's that behind your back?" she asked.

"This?" Wisp pulled her hands out. In one she held a long key with a fancy top. "Nothing. Just a key," she said.

"A key to what?" asked Tink.

Wisp didn't say anything. Her eyes darted toward Vidia's bed.

Vidia gasped. She raced over to the bed and pulled out the locked box of fairy dust. "Give me the key!" she demanded.

Wisp handed it over. With unsteady hands, Vidia slid the key into one of the padlocks. There was a click, and the

lock popped open. She tried the key on another lock. It worked on that one, too.

One by one, Vidia opened all six padlocks.

"Where did you get a key that opens every lock?" Tink asked.

"The keyhole-design talents gave it to me," said Wisp.

Tink frowned. "Why would they give you a key like that?"

"I won a dare," Wisp said. "They bet I wouldn't jump from a branch with one wing tied behind my back. I sure showed them!"

Vidia was barely listening. Slowly, she opened the top of the box. Inside lay the gleaming pile of fairy dust. She could see the mark where Wisp had scooped out a handful.

"You stole from me!" she shouted.

"So?" said Wisp. "You stole feathers from Mother Dove."

Then Vidia thought of something else. "You cheated in our race today!"

"You cheated, too," Wisp pointed out.

Vidia was so mad she was shaking. But she couldn't argue. Wisp might be a thief and a cheat, but after all, so was Vidia.

Vidia was more than just angry, though. She was also hurt and disappointed. She had thought Wisp was her friend. But it turned out that Wisp had only wanted her fairy dust. All Wisp cared about was flying faster.

Just like Vidia.

"Don't be upset, Vidia," Wisp said. "Now that we're both so fast, our races will be better than ever!"

Vidia drew herself up proudly. "You're right," she said. "We need to find out who's the best, once and for all."

"You're racing again?" Tink asked

in disbelief. She turned to Vidia. "You don't have to prove that you're faster than she is."

"You don't get it, Tink," Vidia replied. "You're not a fast flier." The only way to get back at someone like Wisp was to beat her. No one understood that as well as Vidia.

"We'll fly once around Pixie Hollow," she said to Wisp. "First one back to the sour-plum tree is the fastest fairy in Pixie Hollow."

Wisp grinned. "You're on," she said.

Outside, it was dark. Between the leaves of the sour-plum tree, Vidia saw stars twinkling in the night sky.

"On your mark," said Wisp. The two fairies crouched down. "Get set. . . . Go!"

Vidia tore into the air. She imagined herself slicing through it like a knife slicing honey bread. *I'm an arrow,* she thought. *I'm a hawk. I'm the fastest thing in Never Land.*

She would beat Wisp this time. She had to.

With the special fairy dust, Vidia and Wisp flew twice as fast as usual. Trees, rocks, and flowers were just blurs in the darkness. Something stung Vidia's arm, and she realized she'd grazed a leaf. At this speed, even the smallest objects were dangerous.

She was glad when they made it

through the orchard. The open meadows were safer at night. There weren't any trees to hit.

Vidia and Wisp zoomed toward Spring Meadow. Even in the dark, Vidia could see the area that had burned. The air smelled of wet ashes.

Wisp reached the meadow first. As she tore over a blackened patch, Vidia heard a whoosh, then a crackle. An orange flame spurted up from the ground.

Vidia screeched to a halt. She hovered and looked closer. Now she could see what the darkness had concealed at first—the fire was still smoldering. Threads of smoke rose from the burnt ground.

*If we fly over it, we'll start the fire again!* Vidia thought.

"Stop!" she yelled to Wisp. "Get out of the meadow! Your wings are fanning the fire!"

But Wisp didn't stop. She zoomed over the meadow, and more flames sprang up behind her.

"Wisp!" Vidia screamed again, thinking she hadn't heard. "Stop!"

This time Wisp glanced back over her shoulder. When she saw the line of fire rushing toward her, she grinned. "Come on, Vidia!" she called. "Race the flames!"

*She thinks it's a game,* Vidia thought. *Just like the waves. And the arrows. And the hawk. Everything is a game to her.*

But this was one game Vidia wasn't going to play. She didn't care if Wisp won the race, or if she was the fastest fairy in Pixie Hollow.

Wisp wasn't really fearless. She was just foolish.

As Wisp tore across the meadow, the fire chased her. The faster she flew, the higher the flames climbed. They sent sparks shooting into the dry meadow grass. Where they landed, new ground began to burn.

*She'll burn the whole meadow*, Vidia thought. *She'll burn down all of Pixie Hollow!*

Vidia took off after her. She meant to cut Wisp off. But she didn't get far. A blast of smoke and heat drove her back.

Vidia watched the leaping fire quickly circle the meadow. It raced ahead of Wisp, cutting her off. Wisp turned to go back the way she'd come, but another wall of flames blocked her.

Wisp was trapped.

# 10

VIDIA HEARD SHOUTS behind her. Tinker
Bell and the other pots-and-pans fairies
flew up. They had spotted the fire from
the Home Tree.

"It's even bigger than before!" Tink
exclaimed. Then she saw Wisp. "What's
she doing out there? Doesn't she know
it's dangerous?"

Vidia just shook her head. It was too much to explain. More fairies were rushing toward them—water talents, garden talents, animal talents. Everyone had come to help with the fire.

Vidia turned to leave. There was no point in sticking around to get burned up, too.

But as she spread her wings, Vidia paused. Maybe she remembered the fun she'd had racing Wisp. Or maybe it was just that Vidia wasn't as heartless as everyone thought. For whatever reason, Vidia turned back to the fire.

The pots-and-pans fairies formed a chain with water buckets. Someone thrust a bucket into Vidia's hands. She threw the water on the fire. But the thimble-sized bucket only held a few drops. It had no effect on the blaze.

Vidia could see Wisp hopping around. She was still searching for an escape. But it was impossible to fly now. The smoke was too thick, and the sparks were too dangerous. Vidia caught a glimpse of Wisp's face between the flames. For the first time ever, Wisp looked terrified.

*It serves her right*, Vidia thought angrily. *She got herself into this mess. She can get herself out*. Wisp's eyes met Vidia's. Vidia could almost see her asking for help.

Vidia tossed her long ponytail. *I can't just leave her*, she decided.

She looked around. Fairies shouted

to each other. Water talents hurled water balls at the fire. Animal talents herded the meadow creatures to safety.

Then Vidia noticed the animal-talent fairy Fawn. She was coaxing a confused groundhog out of his hole. Watching her, Vidia got an idea.

She flew over to Fawn. "That groundhog tunnel. How far does it go?" Vidia asked.

"Huh?" Fawn looked up from the groundhog.

Vidia wanted to shake her. Why were all fairies so stupidly slow? "The tunnel you just came out of!" she yelled. "Does it go under the whole meadow?"

"Yes, most of it," Fawn said, finally understanding.

"Is there an entrance over there?" Vidia asked. She pointed to the part of the meadow where Wisp was trapped.

"Yes." Fawn nodded. "A small one, I think. More like an airhole."

"Tell me how to get there from here," Vidia commanded.

Fawn scrunched up her face. "Start straight. Turn left at the second fork. Turn right. Then it's on your left. I *think* that's the way, at least."

"It had better be," Vidia snarled. If she got lost in the groundhog tunnels and roasted like a potato, she would blame Fawn.

Vidia dove into the entrance. The tunnel near Mother Dove's nest was always cool, but this one was hot from the fire overhead. It also smelled musty, like groundhogs.

"'Straight . . . left at the second fork . . . ,'" Vidia repeated. She wanted to speed. But the only light she had was her glow. She had to fly slowly so that she wouldn't miss a turn.

Vidia crept through the tunnel. She came to a fork. But was it the first or second? She wasn't sure.

Stuck in the hot, dark, airless tunnel, Vidia started to panic.

"Stop it!" she told herself. She pushed down the panic and moved on. At last she came to what she thought was the right hole. It was tiny, and covered by grass. If Fawn's directions were good, Wisp should be right overhead.

Then again, if they weren't good, Vidia might be roasted to a crisp.

Vidia took a deep breath and flew upward. She heard the flames crackling. When she poked her head out, the heat felt like a blast from an oven.

Right away, she saw Wisp. She was clinging to the only patch of grass that hadn't yet burned.

"Vidia?" Wisp cried. She looked as if she couldn't believe her eyes. "You came to save me?"

Vidia grabbed her hand. "Come on, before I change my mind," she said.

Vidia and Wisp squeezed through the hole and hurried back along the tunnel. They couldn't even fly. Wisp's wings were too scorched.

Finally, they felt cooler air. Vidia and Wisp crawled out of the tunnel, gasping for breath. Vidia closed her eyes and swallowed hard. They had made it. They were safe.

She led Wisp to a patch of moss and told her to lie down. "I'll get a nursing fairy," Vidia said.

But Wisp grasped at her hand. "Will I ever be able to fly again?" she asked.

Vidia snorted. "You'll be fine," she said, shaking her hand free. "I've seen worse wingburns from a candle flame."

"I shouldn't have stolen your fairy dust," Wisp said. She was crying now. "I'd fly backward if I could. I was a fool to keep racing like that. I owe you my life, Vidia."

Vidia's face twisted into a smirk. "Your life?" she said. "And what would I want with a silly thing like that? After all, you're just a foolish little fairy. Only the second-best flier in Pixie Hollow."

Then, with a toss of her long hair, Vidia headed off to find the nursing talent. She flew at just the right speed to keep from fanning the flames, as only the very best fast-flying fairy could.

Don't miss any of the magical
Disney Fairies chapter books!

# Beck Beyond the Sea

"This is your chance, Beck. Fly away. See the world. Go! Go! Go!"

With that, Vidia threw a handful of sparkling dust into the air. The dust twinkled as it rained down on Beck's head and shoulders.

Beck felt a jolt of power surge through her wings. It lifted her through the air and shot her forward toward the flock. It was like a dream. Never had she flown so fast. Never had it been so easy.

She was gaining on them. She could catch up. And once she caught up, she would keep up. *I'm going!* Beck decided in a burst of joy. *I'm going!*

# Queen Clarion's Secret

Just as Prilla was about to land, a shadow crossed the ground in front of her. She looked up and her eyes widened. A huge bird was soaring across the sky. It was unlike any bird Prilla had ever seen. The bird was as colorful as a parrot, but it was much longer. Its wingspan was as wide as an eagle's.

The bird traveled so fast that it left a multi-colored streak in the sky behind it. Prilla felt a shiver of fear. A bird so big and fast could be dangerous to fairies. She would have to warn the queen.

But when she looked back, Queen Clarion was gone.

# Myka Finds Her Way

Myka had to get closer. She had to see what was happening. She flew toward the noise and lights. The rumblings turned to roars. The flashes grew brighter.

Everything looked strange in the on-again, off-again flare of light. *Boom!*

She saw a gnarled tree bent over, its bare branches sweeping the ground. *Boom!* She spotted a towering beehive. It swayed from the thick trunk of a maple tree.

She swerved around it and kept flying. *Boom!* The spooky light cast long shadows from trees . . . plants . . . rocks. Everything seemed different. But she was a scout. She had to keep going.